Ruby Tuesday Readers

Monster Mo's BIG Party

By Dee Reid

Reading Consultant: Beth Walker Gambro

Ruby Tuesday Books

Published in 2018 by Ruby Tuesday Books Ltd.

Copyright © 2018 Ruby Tuesday Books Ltd.

Design and illustrations: Emma Randall
Editor: Ruth Owen
Production: John Lingham

Library of Congress Control Number: 2018946146
Print (hardback) ISBN 978-1-78856-052-8
Print (paperback) ISBN 978-1-78856-070-2
eBook ISBN 978-1-78856-053-5

Printed and published in the United States of America.

For further information including rights and permissions requests, please contact our Customer Services Department at 877-337-8577.

It was Mo's birthday.

"You must have a pink party," said Megan.

Nice!

OK.

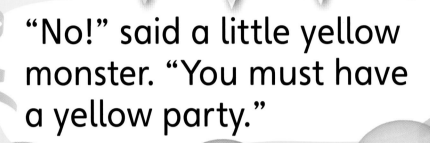

"No!" said a little yellow monster. "You must have a yellow party."

"You must have a rainbow party!" said Molly.

Yes!

21

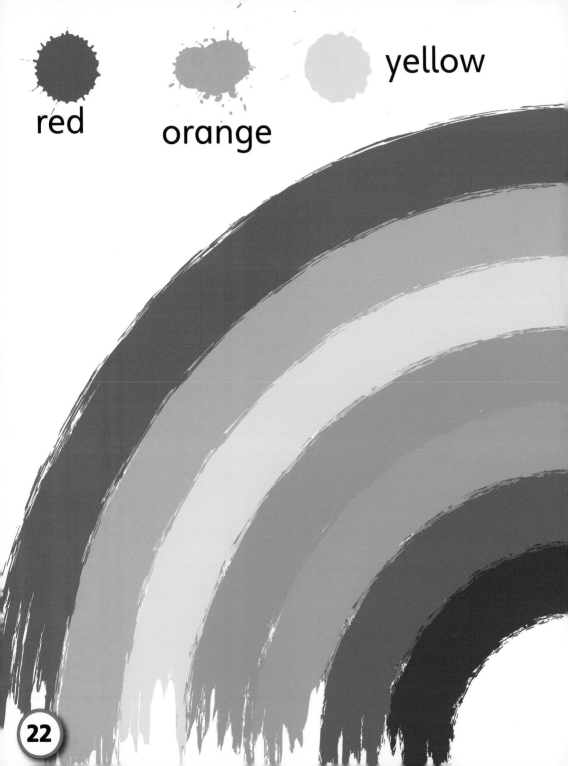

red

orange

yellow

green

blue

indigo

violet

Do you know the colors
of the rainbow?

Can you remember?

Why did Mo have a party?

What color balloons did the little monsters suggest?

Why couldn't Mo make up his mind?

What was Molly's good idea?

Can you read these words?

a   and   have

said   will   you